THE AGRA BOX CASE

A FURTHER SHERLOCK HOLMES ALPHABET

AGRA FORT

By P. James Macaluso Jr.

For Steve Emecz

Analysis

Bewildered
Client

Disappearance

10

Epistle

Fine Gemstones

Handwritten Invitation

Knavery

Leering
Malevolence

Notation

Oriental
Poison

Queer Ruffians

Scent
Trail

Urchins

Visitors

Waterway eXpedition

Yarn

Zilch

Notes on the text

A. The novel begins, like many other stories in the canon, at 221B Baker Street, with Sherlock Holmes demonstrating his acute powers of observation and deduction, this time concerning a pocket watch that Dr John Watson has recently inherited from his elder brother.

BC. In Chapter II, Miss Mary Morstan, whose employer Sherlock Holmes once assisted, visits Baker Street seeking guidance regarding a baffling domestic affair.

D. Miss Morstan states the facts surrounding the mysterious disappearance of her father, Captain Arthur Morstan, from the Langham Hotel upon his arrival in London from India nearly ten years ago.

E. The young lady then proceeds to tell Sherlock Holmes and Dr Watson about the arrival six years ago of a small parcel containing a valuable gift, subsequent to answering an anonymous advertisement in the 'Times' newspaper requesting her address.

FG. Miss Morstan goes on to relate that every year since then, upon the same date, a similar box has arrived containing a similar gift, a large lustrous pearl, without any clue as to the sender.

HI. Finally, Miss Morstan states that earlier that very day she received an invitation, which on the basis of handwriting analysis Holmes concludes was written by the same person who sent the pearls, to meet at the Lyceum Theatre that evening to have restitution for some unknown injustice she has suffered.

J. In Chapter III, Sherlock Holmes and Dr Watson accompany Miss Morstan to the scheduled rendezvous at the theatre and then, after encountering a waiting coachman, to an unknown destination, during which time the young lady shows the detective a diagram, which belonged to her father, of a large building with four names, including that of a certain Jonathan Small, written beside it.

K. In Chapter IV, the party arrives at the home of Thaddeus Sholto, the benefactor that has sent the pearls, who relates the deathbed confession of his father, Major John Sholto, who not only concealed the truth about the untimely death of Miss Morstan's father, but also withheld the young lady's fair share of the immense Agra treasure, which the two men appropriated in India.

LM. Thaddeus Sholto then goes on to recount that as the senior Sholto was about to reveal the location of the hidden treasure to his twin sons, Thaddeus and Bartholomew, a cruel face staring out of the darkness was seen at the window, which completely unnerved the major and resulted is his final demise.

N. In Chapter V, Holmes and company travel to the home of Bartholomew Sholto, whom they find dead behind the locked door of his study, along with a note bearing the inscription 'The sign of the four', the same mark as that left on a piece of paper found upon the chest of Major Sholto after his death six years ago.

OP. Upon initial examination of the chamber, Sherlock Holmes discovers, in addition to a peculiar stone-headed club, a long, sharp, dark thorn, which was used to administer a powerful poison, stuck in the skin just above the ear of the deceased Bartholomew Sholto.

QR. In Chapter VI, as Thaddeus Sholto summons the police, Holmes examines the room more carefully, discovering two sets of odd footprints, one belonging to a wooden-legged man and the other to a small bare-footed individual, who absconded with the Agra treasure that Bartholomew Sholto found secreted in a sealed-up attic space.

ST. In Chapter VII, Holmes and Watson enlist the assistance of Toby, a trained scent hound, to track through the streets of London the two thieves, one of whom had the misfortune to tread in a pungent tar-like substance in the garret of the Sholto residence while making good his escape.

U. In Chapter VIII, after Toby leads Holmes and Watson to a empty riverside wharf, the detective employs the services of the Baker Street Irregulars, a band of street urchins or homeless children, to search for the missing steam launch which the two confederates, now known to be Jonathan Small and a native from the Andaman Islands, have engaged to flee London with the treasure.

V. In Chapter IX, as Watson waits at Baker Street for word about the steam launch *Aurora* from the Irregulars, inspector Athelney Jones of Scotland Yard arrives followed by an unknown visitor, which turns out to be Sherlock Holmes, who has been out, disguised as an aged mariner, tracking the movements of Jonathan Small and his murderous associate.

WX. In Chapter X, upon discovering the escape plan of the two fugitives, Holmes, Watson and representatives of Scotland Yard lie in wait for them in a police boat, culminating in a nighttime chase down the River Thames and the eventual capture of Jonathan Small and the death of Tonga, the Andaman Islander.

Y. In Chapter XI, Jonathan Small is taken to Baker Street, where he recounts the long an involved tale of the Agra treasure and the conspiracy of 'The Sign of the Four', which entails murder, robbery, betrayal and revenge.

Z. Towards the end of the novel, Watson delivers the sought after iron box, which was seized from Jonathan Small, to the home of Mary Morstan, only to learn that the box is empty and the great Agra treasure lies at the bottom of the Thames, while Holmes is left without recognition for his work in the case as Scotland Yard takes all the official credit.

Other books by the author

A BASKERVILLE CURSE: In this volume, Sherlock Holmes's most famous case, *The Hound of the Baskervilles,* is retold in just twenty-six words, wherein the first word begins with A, the last with Z, and the story proceeds as the alphabet progresses. The text is accompanied by amusing photographic illustrations of custom designed LEGO® models and minifigures.

Other books by the author

A SHELROCK HOLMES ALPHABET: Selected characters and objects featuring in the Sherlock Holmes stories written by Arthur Conan Doyle are presented in rhyming verse, from A to Z, and accompanied by amusing photographic illustrations of custom designed LEGO® models and minifigures.

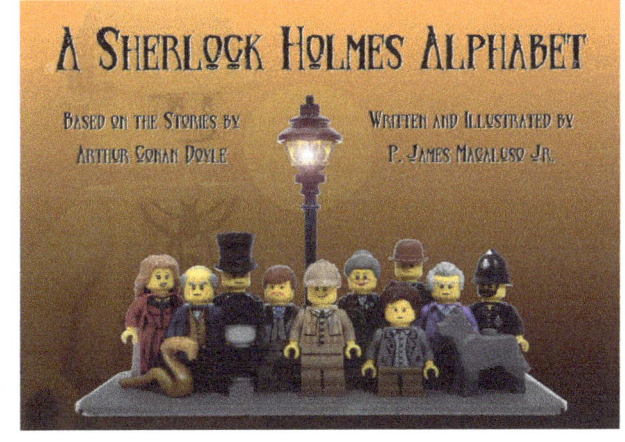

Other books by the author

SHERLOCK HOLMES RE-IMAGINED: The original Sherlock Holmes stories delightfully illustrated using only LEGO® minifigures and bricks. There are 15 individual books in the series, as well as a complete edition that combines the first 12 stories into a single volume.

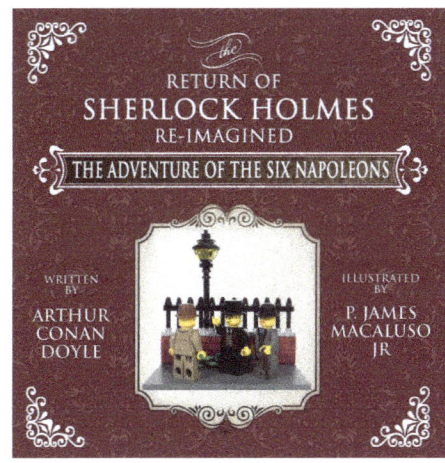

Other books by the author

THE LOST WORLD RE-IMAGINED: The original and unabridged text of Arthur Conan Doyle's science fiction classic accompanied by sixty-five charming color photographic illustrations featuring custom designed models built using only LEGO® brand minifigures and bricks.

Other books by the author

THE LEGEND OF SLEEPY HOLLOW RE-IMAGINED: The original and unabridged text of Washington Irving's ghostly tale accompanied by twenty-eight charming color photographic illustrations featuring custom designed models built using only LEGO® brand minifigures and bricks.

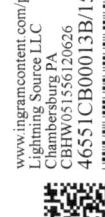